MANU AND THE TALKING FISH

To Debbie and Michael

Barefoot Books
37 West 17th Street
4th Floor East
New York, New York 10011

This book is printed on 100% acid-free paper

This book was typeset in Gill Sans
The collage pictures in this book were made from painted and printed papers.
Watercolor, oil pastel, crayon, and stencilled monoprints were used to make the
patterned designs.

Graphic design by Design Principals, England
Color separation by Grafiscan, Italy
Printed and bound in Hong Kong by South China Printing Co. (1988) Ltd.

U.S. Cataloging-in-Publication Data (Library of Congress Standards)

Arenson, Roberta.
       Manu and the talking fish / written and illustrated by
Roberta Arenson.—1st ed.
[32]p. : col. ill. ; cm.
Summary: The ancient Indian story of Manu, who is
rewarded when he saves the life of a little fish. The fish tells
him what he must do to save himself and the world from
destruction in the coming flood.
ISBN 1-84148-032-0
1. Svarocisa Manu (Hindu mythology) — Folklore. 2. Folk
literature, Indian. 1. Title.
398.2 —dc21 2000 AC   CIP

1 3 5 7 9 8 6 4 2

MANU AND THE TALKING FISH

Written and illustrated by

Roberta Arenson

BAREFOOT BOOKS

A long time ago in India lived a prince called Manu.
Manu often wondered about the mysteries of the world around him. He wondered why the wind blew.
He wondered where the sun slept at night, and he wondered what the birds were singing about.

Every day, Manu went down to sit by
the River Ganges and think. One day,
as he sat by the river, he heard a voice.
"Help me," the voice cried.
Manu looked around, but he could see
no one.

"Help me," the voice called again. Then,
with a sudden splash, a little fish poked
his head up out of the water.
"Please help me. A big fish is chasing me
and wants to have me for his supper!
If you help me, I will help you in return."

Manu sprang to his feet and scooped the fish up out of
the river and into a small bowl. He filled the bowl with
water and carried the fish home to his palace.

"So," said Manu, "how can a little fish like you help me?
Look around at my palace – what help do I need?"

The fish gave a little chuckle, for he was really the god Brahma in disguise. "You have often wondered about the mysteries all around you," he said. "Not only am I a talking fish, but I can see the future. If you promise to keep me alive, I will tell you about all these things."

Manu was very curious about his future, so he gave the fish his promise.

The fish soon grew too big for the small bowl.
He asked to be moved to a larger one and then to an even
bigger one. When he had grown too big for all the bowls in
the palace, he asked to be taken back to the River Ganges.

As time passed, even the River Ganges could no longer hold the fish. "Please take me to the sea," the fish said, and Manu kept his promise.

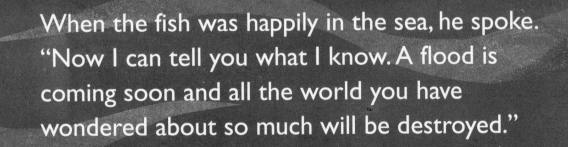

When the fish was happily in the sea, he spoke. "Now I can tell you what I know. A flood is coming soon and all the world you have wondered about so much will be destroyed."

"First you must build a large boat. Then you must gather seeds from all the trees and plants you can find and gather up all the birds and the animals, and tell the seven wise men from the ends of the earth to be ready to go with you."

Manu set about building his boat. It had to be big enough to carry everything.

Then he gathered the seeds and bulbs of
many kinds of trees and fruit and vegetables.

And Manu called to every animal to come with him. There were lions and elephants, snakes and birds, monkeys and cows, giraffes and turtles. And the seven wise men came from the ends of the earth as well.

On the day that Manu finished the
boat, it began to rain. It rained
and it rained and it rained.
Everything was covered by the
water. Everything but Manu's boat,
which was carried out to sea.
The giant fish, which was now
bigger than the boat, called out
from the sea to Manu. "Tie a rope
to my back and I will guide you."
While the waves crashed all
about them, the fish easily pulled
Manu's boat along.

Many days passed and many nights too, but Manu could not tell the difference because there was no sun or moon or stars. It rained all the time and everything was dark.

Finally, the boat came to rest on the highest mountain peak. The fish instructed Manu to tie the boat to the tree at the top of the mountain.

At long last, the rain stopped
and the sun came out.
The waters began to go down.
The giant fish spoke to Manu again.

"I must leave you now,
but come to the sea
after you have settled
and built a new home."

Manu planted all the seeds and
bulbs he had carried on his boat.
He set the animals free and built
a new home.

Then he and the seven wise
men offered thanks to the
gods with milk and cheese.

One day, a beautiful woman
arose out of the milk, and
she became Manu's wife.

They had many children together and so
filled the earth once more with people.

Manu was often seen sitting by the edge of the sea. He sat quietly, listening to the sound of the waves and the wind. Or maybe he was listening to the wise voice of his old friend, the talking fish. What do you think?

ARTIST'S NOTE

Tales of a deluge or flood are found in the literature and oral traditions of almost every culture. They tell of a time when the earth is suddenly covered by water, when the old is washed away so the new can emerge.

Manu and the Talking Fish is my retelling of the ancient Indian deluge story from Hindu mythology. I first came across the Manu tale in Veronica Ions' *Indian Mythology*, and this particular account became the source for my own adaptation of the story. In this version, it is the god Brahma who is disguised as the talking fish. In variations of this myth, it is the god Vishnu who takes on this disguise.

At least two sources from classical Indian literature contain stories of Manu and the flood. According to *Funk & Wagnalls Standard Dictionary of Folklore, Mythology and Legend*, versions of the tale are found in the *Sataphatha Brahamana* and the *Mahabharata*. The tale of Manu predates that of his Biblical counterpart, Noah.

I am fascinated by the Hindu concept of time. The universe is conceived as evolving through vast cycles of creation and destruction, wherein a single day, or *kalpa*, is the equivalent of 4,321,000,000 years. During each kalpa, fourteen floods occur. According to tradition, it is the hero Manu who survives each of these floods and initiates the renewal of life. Heinrich Zimmer, in his illuminating *Myths and Symbols in Indian Art and Civilization*, has noted that the interval between each flood, called a Manvantara, is named after Manu.

In creating the illustrations for the book, I looked at many wonderful examples of art from India. The books *Arts of India* (John Guy and Deborah Swallow, ed.) and *The Arts of India* (Basil Gray, ed.) were excellent sources. I was inspired by *Authentic Folk Designs from India* (K. Prakash) and *5,000 Designs and Motifs from India* (Ajit Mookerjee, ed.) in the creation of my own painted and printed patterns for the book.

While borrowing from Indian motifs, my aim was not to imitate traditional Indian art, but rather to incorporate it into my own style. I am drawn to the rich wardrobes, flowing patterns and decorative elements in the paintings of this ancient culture. They were a lively springboard for the shapes, colours and design elements of my collages.

Through retelling this tale, I hope to share the sense of wonder and mystery I experience with this story — with its age-old universal themes of time, creation and renewal.

Sources

Indian Mythology, Veronica Ions, P. Bedrick Books, 1973.

Funk & Wagnalls Standard Dictionary of Folklore, Mythology and Legend, Maria Leach, ed., and Jerome Fried, Assoc. Ed., Harper & Row, 1949.

Myths and Symbols in Indian Art and Civilization, Heinrich Zimmer, Princeton University Press, 1946.

5,000 Designs and Motifs from India, Ajit Mookerjee, ed., Dover Publications, 1996.

Arts of India, John Guy and Deborah Swallow, ed., Victoria & Albert Museum, 1990.

The Arts of India, Basil Gray, ed., Cornell University Press, 1981.

Authentic Folk Designs from India, K. Prakash, Dover Publications, 1995.